FINAL INNING,
BASES LOADED . . .

It was time to get down to business. Melissa gave Otis a secret signal. She rubbed her sleeve and pulled her left earlobe twice.

Otis nodded behind the catcher's mask. He knew that meant fastball. He held up his mitt.

Melissa wound up, pumped out one leg and fired a rocket over the plate.

Bat Man swung. Too late.

Melissa ground the ball in her mitt. She stared at Bat Man until he looked away. Then she snuck another fastball right past him.

Melissa *had* to strike him out. The game was on the line!

Bantam Skylark Books you will enjoy
Ask your bookseller for the books you have
  missed

THE BLUE-NOSED WITCH
    by Margaret Embry
THE DINOSAUR PRINCESS AND OTHER
    PREHISTORIC RIDDLES
    by David A. Adler
ENCYCLOPEDIA BROWN TRACKS
    THEM DOWN by Donald J. Sobol
THE GHOST SHOW (Annie K.'s Theater
    #2) by Sharon Dennis Wyeth
THE GREEN SLIME (Skylark Choose Your
    Own Adventure #6) by Susan Saunders
I'LL MEET YOU AT THE CUCUMBERS
    by Lilian Moore
JACK GALAXY, SPACE COP
    by Robert Kraus
THE MIGHTY DOLPHIN (Annie K.'s
    Theater #4) by Sharon Dennis Wyeth
THE MUFFIN FIEND by Daniel Pinkwater
SON OF FURRY by Jovial Bob Stine
THE TWINS AND THE WILD WEST
    (Sweet Valley Kids #10) created by
    Francine Pascal

THE NEVER SINK NINE

Major-League Melissa

BY GIBBS DAVIS

Illustrated by
George Ulrich

A BANTAM SKYLARK BOOK
NEW YORK • TORONTO • LONDON • SYDNEY • AUCKLAND

RL 2, 005–008

MAJOR-LEAGUE MELISSA

A Bantam Skylark Book / April 1991

*Skylark Books is a registered trademark of Bantam Books, a division
of Bantam Doubleday Dell Publishing Group, Inc. Registered in
U.S. Patent and Trademark Office and elsewhere.*

ISBN 0-553-15866-X

Published simultaneously in the United States and Canada

---

*Bantam Books are published by Bantam Books, a division of Bantam Double-
day Dell Publishing Group, Inc. Its trademark, consisting of the words
"Bantam Books" and the portrayal of a rooster, is Registered in U.S. Patent
and Trademark Office and in other countries. Marca Registrada. Bantam
Books, 666 Fifth Avenue, New York, New York 10103.*

PRINTED IN THE UNITED STATES OF AMERICA

CWO   0 9 8 7 6 5 4 3 2 1

*For my Aunt Sally, whose
enthusiasm for baseball never
wanes*

CHAPTER ONE

Class Picture Day

Walter Dodd woke up in his team uniform. He had slept in it to make sure it was good and wrinkled, just the way he liked it. He didn't want it to look new for their opening-day game on Saturday.

He poked his feet out from under the covers. He was wearing the lucky socks Grandpa Walt had given him. Walter's grandfather was coach of his baseball team, the Never Sink Nine.

Mrs. Dodd yelled up the stairs.

1

"Last call for breakfast!"

Danny, Walter's older brother, groaned in the bed next to him.

Walter headed for the bathroom. He stepped over a line of tape running along the bedroom floor.

"Watch it," warned Danny. He stared at the floor by Walter's feet. "You're on my side of the line and you know what's going to happen."

Walter froze. "What?"

Danny sat up. He slowly raised a small black pistol from under the covers and took aim.

"No!" shouted Walter, running into the bathroom.

Too late. Danny had shot him in the back with a stream of water.

"I told you I won't go in your stuff again," Walter pleaded from behind the door. "Promise."

"Forget it, you little sneak."

Walter peeked out. "Why won't you believe me?"

"Why should I?" said Danny, pulling on his best pants. He never wore them unless their mother made him.

"Why are you getting so dressed up?" Walter poked his head all the way out.

"Today is picture day, turkey brain."

Walter knew today was special but he had forgotten why. Today was class photo day at Eleanor Roosevelt Elementary.

Danny pointed to a pair of pants and a sweater hanging over a chair. "Mom put those out for you."

Walter got dressed quickly and raced down to breakfast. He had work to do.

Walter shoveled Mrs. Olsen's Oat Bran into his mouth as fast as he could. He studied the offer on the back of the cereal box: an official Babe Ruth wristwatch for twelve box tops. One more and it was his.

Walter loaded his bowl with more oat bran and smashed it down. He poured out the rest.

He waved the empty box in the air. "I need more."

"You want a *third* bowl?" asked Mrs. Dodd.

Walter shrugged. "I'm growing."

Mrs. Dodd searched through the kitchen shelves and set down a new cereal box. Walter ripped off the precious top. He stuffed it in his pocket with the others. He would mail them after school.

Mrs. Dodd stopped Walter on his way out the door. "Let me look at you."

Walter punched his mitt and tried to stand still.

"Promise you'll comb your hair," she said. "Remember your cowlick last year." She pointed to a photo taped to the refrigerator door. One piece of hair stood straight up.

"Promise," said Walter and ran out to his bike.

By the time he rode onto the school playground everyone was inside. Walter was the last one to take his seat.

When I get my new watch I won't be late, he thought.

Mrs. Howard stood at the front of the class. She was wearing her favorite daisy blouse. Small white petals circled her neck. She clapped her hands. Everyone stopped talking.

CLASS PICTURE DAY was written on the blackboard in big letters.

"I must have the best-looking class in school," said Mrs. Howard. "I see *almost* everyone remembered it was picture day." She was looking straight at Walter's best friend, Mike Lasky.

Mike shrunk down behind his desk. He was wearing a faded plaid shirt with paint marks.

Mike leaned across the aisle. "I forgot," he whispered to Walter. His breath smelled like bubble gum—the kind you get inside a pack of baseball cards. He had the best collection in school.

Walter's shirt felt scratchy. He lifted his desk top and looked at his baseball mitt. He wanted to have his picture taken with it.

"I have to leave the room for a few minutes," announced Mrs. Howard. "Who wants to be class monitor?"

Hands shot up.

Walter waved both hands wildly in the air. Class monitor got to sit at Mrs. Howard's desk and use her red pencil. He had never been picked.

A girl with long red hair sitting next to Walter raised her hand.

Melissa Nichols.

Walter looked at her little green horse barettes. How could anyone like horses that much? She had a whole bag of plastic horses.

Mrs. Howard pointed to Melissa. "I'll leave Melissa in charge today."

"Teacher's pet," said Walter so she could hear.

"Jealous," Melissa whispered back.

Walter's ears started to burn. He looked down at the bulging backpack under her chair. Two horses poked out on top. Walter started to kick the bag. Mrs. Howard frowned.

"When I get back we'll line up for class pictures," said Mrs. Howard. "You'll all want to look your best."

Walter and Mike rolled their eyes at each other. Some of the girls were already brushing their hair.

As soon as Mrs. Howard left the room everyone started talking.

Melissa sat behind Mrs. Howard's desk. She put two horses on top. "Be quiet or I'll have to report you," she said, clapping her hands just the way Mrs. Howard did. She held up Mrs. Howard's red pencil for everyone to see.

Walter raised his desk top. "Check this

7

out," he whispered. Taped under the top was a picture of the Babe Ruth watch.

Otis Hooper leaned over to get a closer look. "Big deal," he said.

"Don't you have to send in a ton of box tops?" asked Mike.

"Yeah," said Walter. "Mrs. Olsen's Oat Bran."

Otis stuck a finger down his throat and made a gagging sound. "Who's gonna eat that barfo cereal?"

This was the moment Walter had been waiting for. He held up all twelve box tops.

"Wow!" said Otis and Mike together.

Walter pointed to the picture of the watch. "It's as good as mine."

Melissa clapped her hands. Everyone looked up. "I'm going to report you for talking, Walter Dodd." She made a mark with Mrs. Howard's red pencil.

Walter balled up a piece of paper. "Watch this," he said to Mike. He aimed for Melissa.

"You'd better not," warned Melissa.

"Get her," Mike whispered.

Walter took his best shot. It crashed into the solar system mobile over Mrs. Howard's desk. It was the one he and Grandpa Walt had made for his science project. Mrs. Howard had really loved it. The biggest planet fell to the ground.

"You're in big trouble," said Melissa. She picked up the fallen planet and put it on Mrs. Howard's desk. "You probably won't even get to have your picture taken."

Walter crossed his eyes and stuck out his tongue.

"Watch this, big shot." Melissa picked up the paper ball and aimed for the wastebasket at the back of the room.

"She'll never make it," said Mike.

Walter watched as the ball flew over him in a perfect arc. It dropped right into the center of the wastebasket.

All the girls clapped.

10

Melissa stood up and bowed.

Walter's ears felt hot. He had to work hard at everything—math, reading, even baseball. He had to practice over and over. It wasn't fair. Everything was so easy for Melissa. She was good in school *and* she was the best pitcher the Never Sink Nine had.

Mrs. Howard walked in. "Anything to report?" she asked Melissa.

Melissa held up the fallen planet. She glanced at Walter.

Walter looked down at his desk. His stomach felt funny. He wondered if he'd be sent to the principal's office.

"Jupiter fell," Melissa said. She handed Mrs. Howard the planet.

"Too bad," said Mrs. Howard. She turned to Walter. "Don't worry, Walter. A little glue and your mobile will be good as new."

Walter smiled with relief. He watched Melissa take her seat. Why hadn't she told on him?

Mrs. Howard clapped her hands. "Picture time," she announced. "Line up, please."

Walter took his mitt out of his desk and took his place in line. Mrs. Howard's class walked down the hall single file and stopped outside the gym. Pictures were being taken inside.

Mr. Meyer's third grade class waited in a line next to them.

Mike nudged Walter. "There's Augie Simms." He looked over at a short, pug-nosed boy. The Never Sink Nine was playing the Drill Team on Saturday. Augie was their pitcher.

He looks tough, thought Walter.

He watched Augie sneak up behind a girl wearing ballet slippers. Christy Chung was on Mike and Walter's team. She was brushing her long black hair.

Augie put his fingers across it like scissors. "Snip! Snip!" he said. "Time for a haircut!"

Christy screamed. Her brush went flying. She turned and saw Augie's pretend scissors.

"Very funny," she said, picking up her brush.

Augie looked for another victim.

"Hey, Dodd." Augie looked straight at Walter.

Walter pretended not to hear. He bent down to tie his shoelaces.

"I hear your pitcher's a *giiiirrl*," he said in a high-pitched voice.

Suddenly someone came stomping up the line.

It was Melissa!

"What's wrong with girls, shortie?" She pranced her toy horse across his head.

Everyone laughed—even Augie's team-mates. Augie was the shortest boy in third grade.

Walter watched Augie's face turn bright pink.

"You really cut him down to size," Christy said to Melissa. All the girls congratulated her.

Walter's line moved forward. Mrs. Howard stood at the door calling out names.

"Melissa Nichols."

Melissa stepped forward holding her toy horse.

"You'll have to leave that horse with me," Mrs. Howard said.

Melissa shook her head. "I want my picture taken with Misty."

"I'm afraid that's impossible," said Mrs. Howard.

Melissa tossed her hair back like a horse's mane and stomped the ground with her foot. Her eyes filled with tears.

"All right, all right," said Mrs. Howard, pushing her inside.

Walter was next. He hugged his mitt and tried to make tears come to his eyes.

Mrs. Howard plucked the mitt from his hands. "Leave that with me," she said.

"But I want my picture taken with it."

Mrs. Howard pushed Walter toward the

14

photographer's chair. "Now, hurry it up. We don't have all day."

A light flash went off. Walter rubbed his eyes. All he could see were colored dots. He blinked at Melissa standing in the hall with her girlfriends. Why had she gotten to have her picture taken with her horse? It wasn't fair.

Augie was talking to his teammates. "I'm gonna get her," he said, staring at Melissa.

A shiver went up Walter's spine. Augie was known for his mean tricks.

He looked at Melissa's horse—the one she had her picture taken with.

"She'll be sorry," said Walter. He punched his mitt.

CHAPTER TWO

Boys against Girls

Walter found Mike waiting at the mailbox across from Diamond Park. He was blowing big bubbles with his gum.

"At your service, sir." Mike opened the mailbox door.

Walter held an envelope bulging with cereal boxtops. He checked the address one last time.

MRS. OLSEN'S OAT BRAN
6 MEADOW DRIVE
HILLSIDE, WISCONSIN
ATTENTION: BABE RUTH

For good measure, he had written "Rush" across the top.

"Here goes nothing." Walter tossed the envelope inside.

The mailbox door clanked shut.

"Come on; you'll be late!" Some of Walter's teammates were heading for the Mickey Mantle diamond. It was time for team practice.

Walter and Mike found everyone in the dugout.

A boy with his leg in a cast was taking the Never Sink Nine roll call. Tony Pappas was the best artist in school. He couldn't play this season so Grandpa Walt gave him special jobs to do.

After Tony finished, Grandpa Walt stood up. He was wearing a sweatshirt with COACH written across the front.

"Okay, team. Today is Monday. Opening-day is Saturday," said Grandpa Walt. "The Drill Team is tough but teamwork can beat them. Any questions before we hit the field?"

Melissa whispered something to Christy and raised her hand.

"Walter's cap's on backwards," she said. "That's disrespectful to the team."

All the girls nodded.

Melissa swished her long red braid. It looked just like a horse's tail. Walter felt like giving it a hard pull but Grandpa Walt was watching. Walter punched his mitt instead.

Melissa smiled at the other girls.

"Melissa hogs the whole dugout with her stupid horses," said Walter.

Mike nodded. "She lines them up on the bench and there's no place to sit."

"Yeah!" the other boys chimed in.

Grandpa Walt turned to Melissa. "The dugout bench is for team members, not horses. Okay, Melissa?"

Melissa looked down at her sneakers.

Walter gave the boys a thumbs-up sign.

"One for us," he said.

Grandpa Walt looked at Walter and frowned. "I thought we were a team," he said. "But a *real* team sticks together no matter what. Now we've got work to do before Saturday so let's get started!"

All the players grabbed their mitts and ran to their positions. Walter took second base and Mike took shortstop. Melissa galloped to the pitcher's mound.

Grandpa Walt picked up the biggest bat and stepped up to home plate. He tossed a ball in the air and took one mighty swing.

Crack!

The ball soared over Walter's head into the outfield. Walter felt proud. His grandfather was the best slugger in Diamond Park.

Christy was running for the ball.

"Get it, Christy!" yelled Melissa.

Walter and Mike shook their heads at each other. *It's too far,* thought Walter. *She'll never make it.*

Christy bent her knees like a ballerina and

raised her arms over her head. Then she sprang up and pointed her toes. One arm reached up for the ball.

Plunk!

It landed dead center in her mitt.

The girls cheered wildly.

Christy twirled around like a ballerina.

"Nice work!" shouted Grandpa Walt.

Mike popped a bubble. "Lucky catch."

"Yeah," said Walter. He knew even his lucky socks wouldn't have helped him catch that fly ball.

Walter lifted his mitt. "Throw it in," he said to Christy.

Christy gave him a cold look. She threw it in to Katie at third. Katie threw it to Melissa.

All during practice the girls threw to the girls and the boys threw to the boys. No one was playing together.

Suddenly Christy came marching in from the outfield. She held up her pink ballet slipper.

21

"Look." She waved her slipper in the air. Gum was stuck to the bottom. She pointed to Mike. His face was hidden by a huge bubble. "He's wrecked my shoes!"

Pop! A thin layer of pink covered Mike's face. "I have not!" he said.

"Have too!" Christy shouted back.

· "You wear those dumb shoes everywhere. How do you know you got gum on them here?" said Mike.

Christy pointed to wads of gum dotting the ground around Mike.

"I have gum on my sneakers, too," said Melissa. She stood next to Christy.

"You're lying!" said Walter. He stood next to Mike.

The boys lined up against the girls, shouting and waving shoes in the air.

Suddenly a whistle blew.

Everyone was quiet.

Grandpa Walt walked onto the field. A deep line ran across his forehead.

"I don't know how this started," he said. "But if you can't stop it right now you aren't old enough to be on a team."

No one said anything.

"Now line up for batting practice," said Grandpa Walt. "And no more fighting."

Walter waited for his turn at bat. Billy Baskin was up first. Billy was the team slugger. He cracked three balls into the outfield.

"Wish I could hit like that," said Mike with a sigh. He was next.

Melissa pitched three slow ones. Mike missed two and fouled the last ball.

Mike passed the batting helmet to Walter. "Must be an off day," he said.

Walter tapped the plate with his bat and looked at Melissa. "Ready," he said.

She crossed her eyes and stuck out her tongue.

The first ball flew by.

"Concentrate," said Grandpa Walt.

Walter dug in. He closed his eyes and swung hard.

Zsssst! The ball whistled past his ear.

"Here's a nice *baby* pitch," said Melissa.

Walter gripped the bat tight. He'd show her. The pitch came in, nice and easy.

Swooooosh! His bat cut through the air.

Walter could hear the girls giggling.

"Good try," said Grandpa Walt.

"She made me miss," Walter whispered to the boys behind him.

"No excuses," said Grandpa Walt. "Good players take responsibility for their hits *and* their misses."

One by one the other players took their turns.

"Let's give Melissa a turn at bat," said Grandpa Walt. "I'll pitch and you catch, Walter. Everyone else take the field."

Melissa trotted in from the pitcher's

mound. "One minute, Coach!" She ducked into the empty dugout.

Walter heard her make a soft whinny sound to her horse. He squatted behind home plate and punched his mitt. "We don't have all day!" he yelled.

Melissa stuck her braid up under the batting helmet. She stepped up to the plate and took a practice swing.

Then she hit a grounder to first.

"Here comes a fast one, slugger," said Grandpa Walt.

The ball sailed toward home plate. Melissa swung too early and the ball whizzed over the foul line and bounced into the dugout. Walter chased it under the bench.

Walter could see something move in the corner. "Who's there?" he called.

A pair of red legs disappeared out the side of the dugout. Red was the Drill Team's color.

Why is the Drill Team in our dugout? Walter wondered.

"That's it for today, team!" he heard Grandpa Walt shout across the field.

Everyone ran into the dugout to get their things. Melissa and Katie pranced in together like twin horses.

Suddenly Walter heard a scream. He turned to see Melissa down on her hands and knees. She was looking under the bench.

Grandpa Walt came rushing into the dugout. "What's wrong?"

Melissa looked up at him with tears in her eyes. "My horses!" she said. "They're gone!"

All the girls huddled around her.

"Don't worry, Melissa." Grandpa Walt put a hand on her shoulder. "We'll find them. Come on, everybody. Let's look."

The team looked everywhere—the dugout, the diamond, even the equipment shed.

They found Otis's hidden candy, some soggy baseball cards, and a one-dollar bill, but no horses.

Walter held up the money. "Finders keepers, losers weepers," he said to Mike.

"Let's get some ice cream and celebrate," said Mike.

"Good idea." Walter could already taste chocolate chip ice cream. He tossed his mitt into his backpack and slung it over his shoulder.

Melissa stopped him on his way out. "You were in the dugout," she said. "Did you see anyone take my horses?" She looked straight into his eyes.

"No," Walter said quickly. He ran across the field after Mike. It wasn't *really* a lie. He hadn't seen anyone steal her horses. All he had seen was a pair of red legs.

CHAPTER THREE

Big-Shot Brother

"Hurry up, Walter!" Mike stood on the top step of Eleanor Roosevelt Elementary on Friday morning. "They posted game schedules!"

Walter raced up the school steps. Mike and Walter ran down the hall. A crowd was gathered outside the gym. Everyone was looking at the bulletin board. Walter pushed his way up to the front.

"Babe, Babe, Babe, Babe, Babe." Walter said it five times because five was his lucky number. He crossed all his fingers and looked up at the list.

SATURDAY 10:00   NEVER SINK NINE/
 DRILL TEAM   BABE RUTH DIAMOND

Walter let out a yell. "We got it!" He rubbed the face of his new Babe Ruth watch. It had arrived in the mail this morning. Two lucky signs in one day. They *had* to win now.

Mike poked Walter in the side. Augie and some of the Drill Team were a few feet away. They were laughing and pointing at something on the bulletin board.

What's so funny? thought Walter. He pushed his way closer and stood behind Augie.

"Wonder what the reward is?" said Augie. He didn't seem to notice Walter. "Think it's worth a trip to the equipment shed?"

"Are the horses still there?" asked one of Augie's friends.

"Sure," said Augie. "In the bushes."

Walter watched Augie and his teammates

TRACK MEET TODAY 2PM
BASEBALL SCHEDULE
DRILL TEAM / NEVER SINK NINE
BABE RUTH DIAMOND
N

move away. They walked down the hall hitting each other on the back. They were still laughing.

Walter moved closer. He read the notice.

"It *was* Augie," Walter said to himself.

"What?" said Mike.

The school bell rang.

"Come on," said Walter. "We'll be late." He started for their homeroom. "We're getting the class pictures back today!"

As soon as they sat down, Mrs. Howard passed out the pictures. "Put them away," she said.

Walter took one look at his and shoved it in his desk. He hated it. His cowlick stood straight up and he had no mitt.

"Time for lunch," said Mrs. Howard.

Walter was last in the cafeteria line. Friday was fish day. Walter pushed the fishsticks off his plate and loaded up on cherry Jell-O.

All the boys from the Never Sink Nine sat together. The girls sat at the table across from them. Everyone was passing around class pictures.

Walter looked over at Melissa. She was staring at her picture—the one with her and Misty. *She misses that dumb horse,* thought Walter. He wondered if he should tell her about Augie. Walter thought about how it felt when his lucky socks were gone.

He jabbed his Jell-O with a fork.

"Let's see your picture," Mike said to Walter.

Walter pulled his picture out of his pocket. "It's crummy," he said. "My mitt isn't in it."

Walter looked over at Melissa. *She probably is crying fake tears,* he thought. *Why should I care if she gets her horses back? Serves her right.*

"Hey, squirt!"

A stream of water hit Walter in the face. Everyone laughed. Walter blotted his eyes. His brother Danny stood in front of him grinning.

Walter didn't know whether to be angry or happy. Everyone knew Danny was the best hitter in the Rockville League. Sometimes it was great having a fourth-grade brother, even if he sometimes squirted you in the face.

"Heard you got your Babe Ruth watch today," said Danny. "Let's see."

Walter took off his watch and handed it to Danny.

Danny strapped it to his wrist. "I'll wear it home for you, okay?"

Danny didn't wait for an answer. He ran off.

Walter felt sick. He didn't care if Danny was his big-shot brother. No one could take his brand-new Babe Ruth watch and get away with it.

This time he was going to fight back.

CHAPTER FOUR

Walter Strikes Back

After school Walter bicycled straight into Rockville. He pulled up in front of Klugman's Drugstore and went inside.

He ran up and down the aisles searching every shelf.

"Can I help you find something, dear?" asked Mrs. Klugman.

"Water pistols," said Walter, out of breath.

Mrs. Klugman led him to a large bin.

Walter dug through a mountain of red, blue, and green water pistols. Then he saw it—

the perfect weapon for little brothers. At the bottom of the bin was a giant orange-glow, double-barreled water pistol.

He pulled it out and squeezed the trigger. What a beauty! It was twice as big as Danny's.

"Perfect," said Walter.

A price tag was stuck to the side. It would take every cent in his pocket. But it would be worth it.

Walter pedaled home at full speed. He had to get there before Danny.

He burst through the front door and started upstairs.

"Walter, is that you?" shouted Mrs. Dodd. "Let me see your class photo!"

Walter groaned. He found his mother in the kitchen making dinner. She wiped her hands and gave him a kiss.

"I can't wait." She held out her hand.

Walter pulled a crinkled picture out from the bottom of his backpack.

Mrs. Dodd took one look and sighed. "Not

again, Walter." She took down last year's photo and taped the new one to the refrigerator. Walter's cowlick stuck straight up from his head, same as last year.

Walter looked at Danny's photo next to it. He had an idea.

"Can I have Danny's old picture?" he asked.

"What for?"

"My picture album," said Walter, sweetly.

"Fine," said Mrs. Dodd. "Don't forget that it's Friday. Grandpa Walt night."

Grandpa Walt came to dinner every Friday.

Good, thought Walter. They could talk about the big game tomorrow.

He ran up the stairs to the bathroom and shut the door.

Walter had to work fast. He turned on the faucet and filled his pistol. He taped Danny's old class photo to the wall above the bathtub.

37

He stood back and raised the killer pistol. "Take this, you dirty dog!"

He aimed and squeezed the trigger. A blast of water blotted out Danny's face.

Walter smiled with satisfaction. He was ready.

Walter hid the pistol under his mattress and waited for Danny. He rubbed his wrist where his new watch should have been. He thought about all the months it took to eat twelve boxes of Mrs. Olsen's Oat Bran. No one else in the family would touch it. He ate every awful bite for the Babe.

"I'm hooooome!" yelled Danny.

Walter heard his brother coming up the stairs toward their bedroom.

Danny opened their door and let out a loud burp. He looked at Walter standing by his bed. "What're you staring at?" he said.

Walter took a deep breath. "Give me back my watch," he demanded.

Danny held up the arm with Walter's watch on it. "Come and get it."

Walter reached for the pistol. He had shoved it too far under the mattress! He tried to pull it out.

Danny took out his small black pistol and squirted him in the back.

Walter struggled with the mattress. He ripped out all the sheets. Danny kept squirting until his pistol was out of water. Walter's shirt was soaking wet.

"Now I know why your team sponsor's a plumbing company," Danny laughed. "You're a bunch of drips!"

Walter finally felt the end of his pistol. He grabbed it, turned and shot a long hard stream into Danny's surprised face. "Take that!" he shouted.

"You'll never get your watch now!" Danny walked into the bathroom to load up. Walter

39

followed him, squirting him all over. It felt great!

Danny took off the watch and dangled it near the running water. "Back off!" he yelled. "Or it dies!"

Walter's eyes opened wide. "No!" he screamed. "My watch!"

Danny looked up over Walter's head. Suddenly he was quiet.

"Turn off that water," said a deep voice behind Walter. Walter turned around. It was Grandpa Walt.

"What's going on here?" he said.

"He took my watch." Walter pointed to Danny.

"Take it, you crybaby." Danny pushed the watch at Walter.

Walter held it in his hand. He had won, but he didn't feel like a winner.

Grandpa Walt looked Danny straight in the eye. "This isn't like you, Danny." He put a

hand on his shoulder. "What's really bothering you? Is it yesterday's game?"

Danny looked away. "My team lost because of me," he said. His voice trembled. "I struck out."

Walter's mouth dropped open. Danny never struck out. He was Danny the Driver. He always won, just like Melissa.

"No one player loses a game, Danny," said Grandpa Walt. "A team wins together and they lose together. Okay, slugger?"

Suddenly Walter's big brother looked more like a little brother. Grandpa Walt gave Danny a big bear hug.

Walter wanted one too but he didn't say anything.

Danny dumped his pistol in the sink. Walter stared at his brother as he walked past.

"Sometimes big brothers have troubles, too," said Grandpa Walt.

Walter didn't answer. He strapped his

watch back on his wrist. He'd never let it go again.

"Dinner!" shouted Mrs. Dodd up the stairs.

"Let's go," said Grandpa Walt. "Better eat up before our big game tomorrow." He started down the stairs. "Race you!" he shouted.

Walter ran after him.

CHAPTER FIVE

The Big Game

Saturday finally came.

Walter woke up in his team uniform. A button had come off during the night. Good. Now his uniform was really broken in.

Today was the big day. The Never Sink Nine's first official game. Walter couldn't wait to get to the Babe Ruth field.

He breathed hard on his new watch. Babe Ruth's face disappeared under a cloud. He rubbed it on his sleeve and checked the time.

The little bat pointed to six. The big bat pointed to three. 6:15.

The game didn't begin until ten o'clock. Almost four whole hours. Walter wondered what Babe Ruth would do if he had four hours to go.

Walter pulled his mitt out from under his pillow and slipped off the rubber band. A baseball sat snugly inside the pocket. He took it out and gave the mitt a good hard punch.

It was breaking in just right.

Walter looked over at the other bed. Danny was sound asleep. Walter tiptoed across the line on the floor. His lucky socks were under Danny's uniform. He had been putting them there every night to soak up Danny's hitting power. He grabbed them and raced back to his side of the room.

Walter held the socks up to his face and breathed in.

They didn't smell lucky yet.

What if Danny wasn't lucky anymore?

Maybe when he lost his game he lost his luck, too.

"Lucky, lucky, lucky, lucky, lucky," he said five times for good luck, pulling on the socks.

Danny raised an eyelid. "What time is it?"

Walter checked his new watch. "Six-sixteen on the nose," he said proudly.

Danny whipped out his water pistol and shot him in the face. "That's for waking me up too early," he said and rolled over.

Walter wiped his face on his sleeve and grinned. Now he wouldn't have to wash. Nothing could ruin today. Not even Danny.

Walter was the first player in the dugout. He looked at Babe Ruth's face in his watch. He was a full hour early.

"You'd be early, too. Wouldn't you, Babe?" Walter said.

An old station wagon pulled up beside the dugout. Grandpa Walt stuck his head out the window and waved.

47

Walter waved back. He looked around. All the baseball diamonds were filling up with kids. The Rockville League was warming up.

One by one, the Never Sink Nine entered the dugout.

"Time for roll call," said Grandpa Walt.

Tony looked up from a stack of drawings. All the girls sat on one end of the bench. The boys sat on the other. "Melissa's not here," Tony said and went back to drawing.

"Where is she?" asked Grandpa Walt. "It's not like her to be late."

The Drill Team was gathering in their dugout. Every one of them had the same flattop haircut. *They look like a real team,* thought Walter.

Melissa walked into the dugout and sat down without a word.

Grandpa Walt didn't ask why she was late. "Did you find your horses?" he asked her.

Melissa looked down at her sneakers. She shook her head.

"We looked everywhere," said Christy. "Somebody stole them."

Walter dropped his mitt. He wished they'd stop talking about her stupid horses.

"Okay, everyone. Photo time!" Grandpa Walt called out. He took a photograph of the team before every game. Everyone lined up and Grandpa snapped two shots. Even Melissa managed to smile.

The Drill Team was out on the field. Augie Simms stood on the pitcher's mound. "Come on, slowpokes!" he shouted. "Let's play ball!"

The Never Sink Nine was up at bat first. Katie stepped into the batter's box.

"Give it a ride!" shouted Grandpa Walt.

The girls clapped. The boys pretended they weren't watching.

"Ready or not, here it comes." Augie wound up and fired a low fastball. Katie was ready.

Crack!

It bounced down the third-base line.

The girls jumped up and cheered. "Run, Katie, run!"

Katie made it to first base.

"Crackerjack Katie!" yelled Grandpa Walt.

"Anyone could have hit that ball," Mike mumbled.

Walter smiled nervously. He hoped Augie pitched him a slower one.

"Next victim!" shouted Augie.

No one stepped up to the plate.

"Who's next?" asked Grandpa Walt.

Tony checked the lineup. "Melissa."

"We don't have all day!" shouted Augie.

"Take your time," Grandpa Walt said to Melissa. He handed her a batting helmet.

Melissa dragged the bat to home plate.

"You can do it!" said Grandpa Walt.

Melissa smiled weakly.

Walter heard a noise. He leaned forward. The catcher was *neighing* like a horse!

51

Melissa jumped back and dropped the bat. The ball whizzed past.

"Just *horsing* around!" said Augie. He slapped his leg with his mitt and laughed.

Melissa froze like a statue.

The second ball sailed past.

On the third pitch Melissa didn't even blink.

"Strike three. You're *out!*" shouted the umpire.

"Don't worry. You'll get 'em next time," said Grandpa Walt.

Melissa didn't answer. She sank down on the bench.

Otis was up next and he struck out. Then Billy hit a fly ball that the center fielder caught easily.

"Our turn to take the field," said Grandpa Walt. "Come on, Melissa."

Walter watched her walk out to the pitcher's mound. She used to gallop. Walter ran to second base.

Melissa walked the first two batters. One of them was Augie.

"You pitch like a *girl!*" Augie sneered.

Walter waited for Melissa to shout back. She didn't say a word.

"She's gonna wreck it for us," said Mike.

Walter kept his eye on Augie on second. "I saw your brother's game," said Augie. "Pretty embarrassing. Bet you wish he wasn't your brother."

Walter felt angry. Even though he was angry at his brother, he hated it when anyone else teased Danny.

Augie inched away from the base. He was trying to steal third! He started to run.

Katie was on third base. She saw him coming. "Melissa!" she shouted.

Melissa threw the ball to Katie. Katie reached up for the catch. Augie ran right into her. Katie fell backwards and the ball rolled out of her mitt.

Augie looked down at her. "Stay out of my way next time," he said.

The game went quickly. Walter looked at his watch. Eleven-fourteen. The scoreboard had barely changed.

INNING 4 NEVER SINK NINE 1
DRILL TEAM 2

If it hadn't been for Christy's home run, the score would have been 2-0.

The Never Sink Nine piled into the dugout.

Tony looked at the batting lineup. "Your turn, Walter."

Walter's stomach turned flip-flops. He had struck out twice already. He gave his lucky socks a tug. He needed them now more than ever. He took a deep breath and stepped into the batter's box.

"Look who's up to bat!" shouted Augie. "It's Danny the Strike-Out's brother, Walter the Wimp!"

"Look who's talking!" Walter shouted back. "Simms the Simp!"

Walter gripped the bat tight.

Crack!

He hit a weak grounder in front of home plate.

Walter ran with all his might. Augie scooped up the ball and fired it to first base.

Walter slid into base. A cloud of dust hid his feet.

"Safe!" shouted the umpire.

The Never Sink Nine cheered—boys *and* girls.

It was Melissa's turn at bat.

Walter could tell Augie was going to throw a fastball. Augie fired it high to the right. It hit Melissa on the shoulder. She fell to the ground and grabbed her arm.

"Time-out!" shouted Grandpa Walt, running over to her.

He helped her into the dugout. "You'd

better shape up!" he shouted across the field to Augie.

Augie shrugged. "Sorry."

Walter jogged in from first base. "Are you okay?" he asked Melissa. He wasn't angry at her anymore. Augie had gone too far this time.

Melissa brushed the dust off her uniform and stood up. "I'm okay," she said, holding her arm. She walked away slowly.

Grandpa Walt looked concerned. "I should take her out of the game."

"She's tough," said Mike.

Walter nodded. Mike was right. The Drill Team just *looked* tough. Melissa *was* tough.

Walter looked at Melissa on the dugout bench. He wanted to do something to cheer her up.

Tony handed Melissa one of his drawings. "Here," he said. It was covered with horses.

"Misty," whispered Melissa. "Thanks." She folded it carefully and tucked it in her shirt pocket.

Walter knew it wasn't enough. She needed the real thing. She had to have her horses just like he had to have his lucky socks.

Walter looked at the Never Sink Nine. The girls and the boys sat at opposite ends of the bench. If they were going to win they had to get together.

Walter looked at his watch. His hero's face stared back at him. What would The Babe do?

He walked up to Grandpa Walt. "I need a time-out," he said. "It's important."

"Can't it wait?"

Walter shook his head. He looked into his grandfather's eyes. "It's for the team. We need it to win this game."

"I can't call a time-out unless you're injured," Grandpa Walt said. "But since we're at bat, we can play without you. You've got five minutes, kiddo. I hope you know what you're doing."

Walter raced for the equipment shed. It was up to him now.

CHAPTER SIX

The Horse Play

Walter ran as quickly as he could and turned the corner of the Diamond Park equipment shed. He plunged both arms into a bush and fished around. His hand hit something.

Could it be a toy horse?

He reached in further and pulled out Melissa's backpack.

Walter checked his watch. Three minutes had gone by. He slung the bag over his shoulder and raced back.

Clickety-clack, clickety-clack, clickety-clack.

Two dozen plastic horses tumbled together as he ran across the ballpark.

I have to save time, thought Walter. He cut across the Willie Mays diamond—right through a game!

"Hey, get off our field," yelled a player. Walter snorted like a horse and galloped on by.

The edge of the Babe Ruth diamond came into sight. He was almost there. His legs felt wobbly and his chest ached. He wanted to stop and catch his breath. But he couldn't. His team was already out in the field again.

Walter squinted to see the scoreboard.
INNING 6 NEVER SINK NINE 3
DRILL TEAM 2

Walter looked at his watch. His five minutes were up.

Billy Baskin must have hit a home run!

My team needs me, thought Walter. He pulled up his lucky socks and broke into a run.

Melissa threw a slow pitch. Too slow. It sank to the ground before reaching the batter.

"Ball four," yawned the umpire. "Take your base."

The players on first and second moved ahead. The bases were loaded.

Tony was standing at Walter's position on second base. He raised a crutch in the air as Walter ran past. "Where have you been?"

"Can't talk," Walter said, out of breath.

Grandpa Walt came after him. "I said *five* minutes, Walter."

Walter didn't have time to explain. The bases were loaded, with two out. If Melissa didn't get the next batter out they'd probably lose the game! He disappeared into the dugout.

Everyone was waiting to see who the next batter would be.

A huge boy in a red Drill Team uniform stomped up to home plate.

BAT MAN was written in big letters across his chest. He picked up the longest, heaviest bat and took a practice swing. He was Augie's cousin, the Drill Team's pinch hitter.

Swooooosh!

Melissa wound up to throw the ball. It slipped out of her hand and fell to the ground.

Coach Walt shook his head. "We all tried as hard as we could," he said, looking down at the ground.

Suddenly there came a loud noise from the dugout.

The Never Sink Nine looked over from the field.

Someone was prancing around like a horse in front of the dugout.

It was Walter!

Melissa shielded her eyes from the sun and squinted toward him. Her face burst into a smile and she flew to the dugout.

"Misty!" she shouted.

"Melissa!" Walt shouted. "Get back to the mound." But Melissa kept running.

Lined up on the bench inside were all twenty-four of Melissa's prized horses!

The girls started cheering. Then the boys joined in. The Never Sink Nine was a team again!

Melissa scooped up an armful of horses and hugged them tight. "Where'd you find them?" she asked Walter.

He shrugged. "I'll tell you later. But now we've got a game to win."

Melissa carefully put down each horse. "Will you watch them for me?" she asked Tony as he came in from second base.

"Sure," he said. "Now go break a leg." He tapped his cast.

Melissa laughed. It was the first time Walter had seen her happy since her horses were stolen.

Walter ran out to second base. Melissa trotted right beside him to the pitcher's mound.

"Finished playing with your toys?" said Augie from third base.

Melissa wasn't listening. She flung her cap to the ground and undid her braid. She shook out her long red hair like a horse's mane and stomped her foot on the mound. She tossed her head back and let out a long loud whinny.

The horses have worked their magic, thought Walter. The old Melissa was back. It was time to get down to business. Melissa gave Otis a secret signal. She rubbed her sleeve and pulled her left earlobe twice.

Otis nodded behind the catcher's mask. He knew that meant she would throw her hardest fastball. He held up his mitt.

Melissa wound up, pumped out one leg and fired a rocket over the plate.

Bat Man swung. Too late.

Melissa ground the ball in her mitt. She

stared at Bat Man until he looked away. Then she snuck another fastball right past him.

"Hey, wait a minute," said Bat Man, looking for the ball.

Augie walked over to his cousin and whispered something in his ear.

Bat Man's face broke into a smile. "You'd better watch it," he warned Melissa. "Or your horses are going on a long trip."

Grandpa Walt stepped forward. "You'd better hope they don't, son. Now play ball."

Bat Man gulped. "Yes, sir," he said, looking up at Walter's grandfather. He was big but Grandpa Walt was bigger.

Melissa wound up. It looked like another fastball. Bat Man swung hard.

Swooooosh!

His bat sliced air.

Melissa had tricked him with a slow change-up. Bat Man watched it sail quietly past his shoulder.

Grandpa Walt ran onto the field and gave

Melissa a big hug. Tony threw all his drawings into the air.

"We won!" shouted Walter. He gave Mike a high-five.

The Never Sink Nine rushed onto the pitcher's mound. They all threw their caps and mitts into the air.

Christy leapt off to the side and shouted a new cheer.

"Two, four, six, eight,
  Who's the one the hitters hate?
  Melissa! Melissa! Yeeeeeah, Melissa!"

Everyone joined in and they sang it a second and third time.

Grandpa Walt's station wagon pulled up next to them. "Time for the victory ride," he said. "All aboard!"

Everyone piled in. Walter, Mike, and Melissa sat in the back with the tailgate down. They circled Diamond Park three times.

"Next stop, the Pizza Palace!" announced Grandpa Walt.

Everyone cheered.

The whole team squeezed in at one table. It was Katie's turn to choose pizza. Sausage and mushrooms with extra cheese.

"That last pitch was great," Mike said to Melissa. "What do you call it?"

Melissa shrugged. Then she looked at Misty and her face lit up. "I know," she said. "The horse play."

Everyone laughed.

A few kids congratulated Billy Baskin and Christy on their home runs. Walter thought about his strikeout at the game.

"Wish I could hit a homer," said Walter.

"You made the winning catch at our last game," said Melissa.

She was right. Walter rubbed his socks against his chair. "Just lucky," he said.

Melissa held up one of her horses. "Me, too," she said, smiling at Walter.

68

"I've got some new cards," said Tony. "Wanna see?" He pulled a stack of baseball cards out of his pocket.

"Let's trade," said Mike. "Who do you have?"

"See for yourself." Tony spread them out on the table.

Walter leaned over to see. He couldn't believe it. They were all pictures of the Never Sink Nine!

"I made baseball cards of our team," said Tony. "Just like the major leagues."

The pictures were so good it was easy for all of them to find their own cards.

"Awesome," said Mike. He held up his card. His face looked great without any bubble gum on it.

"These are *great*," said Christy. "You're really good at drawing."

"Even though I couldn't play," said Tony, "I wanted to help the team."

Otis looked at his and frowned. "I look fat."

"You are a little fat," said Mike.

Otis grabbed Mike's pizza out of his hand and stuffed it in his mouth. Mike punched Otis's arm.

Walter couldn't stop staring at his card. At last he had a picture with his mitt.

Grandpa Walt held his card up. "These will really put our team on the map."

"Who do we play next, Coach?" asked Billy Baskin.

"The Polar Blasts," said Grandpa Walt. "They won their game, too."

"We'll *blast* them off the field," joked Melissa.

Grandpa Walt got out his car keys. "Team bus leaves in two minutes."

Everyone raced to the parking lot.

Later that night Walter tiptoed across the bedroom floor. Danny was already in bed. He

71

felt something sticky under his feet and looked down.

The tape was gone!

Danny turned on the light. "Heard you stuck up for me at your game."

Walter started walking the sticky line—heel, toe, heel, toe. "Augie's a real jerk," he said.

"About the line," said Danny. "Don't get used to it. It goes down again first thing tomorrow."

Walter grabbed his mitt off the dresser and got into bed.

"Hey, squirt."

Walter looked over at his brother. Danny's water pistol was pointed staight at him.

"No!" shouted Walter. He pulled the covers over his head.

"Relax. It's lemonade."

Walter's head popped up. Danny was squirting lemonade into his mouth.

Walter leaned over the bed. "I want some." He opened his mouth.

Danny gave him a squirt and turned out the light. "'Night, turkey brain."

Walter settled under the covers with his mitt. What a day. Horses and lemonade. He licked his lips for the last drop.

His watch glowed on his wrist.

"I'm gonna be a home-run hitter like you, Babe," he whispered. "I promise."

ABOUT THE AUTHOR

GIBBS DAVIS was born in Milwaukee, Wisconsin, graduated from the University of California at Berkeley, and lives in New York City. Her first novel, *Maud Flies Solo,* is also a Bantam Skylark book. She has published *Swann Song,* a young adult novel, with Avon Books. *Walter's Lucky Socks* and *Major-League Melissa* are the first two books in The Never Sink Nine series for First Skylark.

ABOUT THE ILLUSTRATOR

GEORGE ULRICH was born in Morristown, New Jersey, and received his Bachelor of Fine Arts from Syracuse University. He has illustrated several Bantam Skylark books, including *Make Four Million Dollars by Next Thursday!* by Stephen Manes and *The Amazing Adventure of Me, Myself, and I* by Jovial Bob Stine. He lives in Marblehead, Massachusetts, with his wife and two sons.